Journaling
F O R Joy

✳ **THE WORKBOOK** ✳

Journaling FOR Joy

✳ THE WORKBOOK ✳

Writing Your Way to Personal Growth and Freedom

A breakthrough lifebook from the author of
LIVE YOUR DREAM

Joyce Chapman, M.A.

ISBN: 0-87877-226-X
First printing 1995
10 9 8 7 6 5 4 3 2 1
Printed in the United States of America.

Edited by Gina Misiroglu
Cover and interior design by Michele Lanci-Altomare
Typeset by Amy Inouye

This book is dedicated to those who dare to be true to themselves and journal for joy.

Table of Contents

Acknowledgments

I WANT TO ACKNOWLEDGE AND THANK ALL THE INCREDIBLE PEOPLE WHO HAVE LEARNED right along with me as we've laughed, cried, shared, and journaled to rediscover our Joy. Thanks especially to my family for their unfailing encouragement and for helping to make this workbook possible. Thank you also to all the journalers who, with open hearts, shared their own growth to enrich this book. Also a note of appreciation to Eva Ditler for her expertise and commitment and to Gina Misiroglu for her marvelous editing skills.

Introduction

WELCOME TO THE ADVENTURE OF YOUR LIFE. *JOURNALING FOR JOY: THE WORKBOOK* IS your takeoff point for one of the most exciting journeys you can ever embark upon— the journey into yourself. On this journey you will be your own personal tour guide. Along the way you will be invited to laugh, cry, remember and let go, to travel through your past, to acknowledge your present, and to create your future. You will take a close look at who you are now and what you want in your life, inviting your deep inner knowing to come forth. You will assume your rightful position as the main character in your own life. You will determine your future out of conscious choice.

Journaling for Joy: The Workbook offers a method of journaling in which you, the journaler, will write from your heart and soul with a single focus: to bring your work to the point where joy emerges. Most of the exercises in this workbook can be done over and over again and, although the workbook has been designed to write in the space provided, whenever you feel motivated to write more, just use your favorite blank journal and write away. No matter how much writing it takes to get there, your explicit purpose and intention is to experience the joy that comes from knowing yourself as an intimate friend, and living the life you have created for yourself out of conscious choice.

Journaling for Joy: The Workbook reveals a special and magical way of molding each of your life's experiences into an outcome of learning and joy. You will move through whatever causes you emotional pain, stress, fear, and confusion until, far back in the distance, you can view it all from the perspective of wisdom and gratitude—as a rich tapestry woven from all the powerful and mundane experiences that have unfolded in your life.

Journal writing invites you to pay serious attention to your life—to ask yourself every day, "Where am I in my life journey right now?" And further: "What is my life telling me right now? Who do I want to be? What do I want? Where do I want to go?"

Self-inquiry and self-discovery will give you more information about yourself than if you had read a whole library of books and consulted countless experts. Journaling will become your tool for self-understanding and will provide a way to discover what is keeping you from feeling healthy, creative, and joyful. Journaling can be the mouthpiece for the inner voice. It becomes a highly personal form of inner work, a work that is yours alone to do. It is the work that brings you home to your own truth, a home where the joy presides.

Whatever the circumstances, whenever an individual keeps a journal, there is a way to live life from choice rather than reaction. There is a way to take the driver's seat in life rather than remaining a passive backseat passenger who does not know the destination and is not paying attention to the route. There is a way to be in charge of life and be joyful.

SOME POINTS TO REMEMBER ABOUT JOURNALING

- Journaling is a natural process.
- The subconscious offers wonderful gifts of truth from the inner self.
- The act of writing makes thoughts become real and brings a deeper level of release than just verbal communication or thinking can do alone.
- Don't stop writing—journal through the negative thoughts and beliefs. You need to write through all the layers of stored emotional and psychological perceptions so that you can heal your past.
- There is no right or wrong way to journal.
- Never judge, censor, or correct your journaling.
- Allow your gut reaction or intuition to come forth.
- Set no performance standards on yourself.
- Cancel out the thought that you can't write well.
- Write for yourself.
- Allow yourself to play—have fun!

COMMON QUESTIONS ABOUT JOURNAL WRITING

I. What, one more thing I have to impose on myself?

Once you begin to reap the rewards of your writing, journaling stops being a burden and often becomes the activity you look forward to most and obtain the greatest value from.

2. I'm afraid someone might read my journal. What should I do about this fear?

Hide your journal, or if you've written something you don't want to keep, throw it away or burn it. Remember, it's your journal and it's perfectly OK to keep it private and do whatever you want with it.

3. What if I tell myself the truth in my journal and become frightened by the changes I see that need to be made in my life?

Respect the self-protective function of fear, but give more power to self-expression and free choice than to the fear. Remember, as remote as it may appear, joy is the other side of fear.

4. Someone told me that journaling can make people emotional, and sometimes even makes them cry. Will that happen to me?

It's true that some people are emotional during the writing process, but being emotional is a healthy, cleansing part of the process. And, of course, everyone experiences the journaling process differently. Emotions and tears may be released (and may need to be released) as the writing taps into deeper undercurrents of the psyche. If these emotions seem too overwhelming, consider seeking professional help.

5. Would I ever want to read all this stuff?

Your writing may simply serve the purpose of clearing out the clutter from your mind—a worthwhile result even if it is never read again. On the other hand, writing that at first seems purposeless may lead to valuable insights as your ideas develop. Rereading your writing later and observing what occupied your mind at a particular time is often very meaningful and instructive.

6. Is there much point in writing down everything that happens every day?

Journaling for Joy: The Workbook is a natural process that goes beyond this kind of routine recording or logging of the day's events. It leads you to examine and extract the feelings and meaning behind your experiences.

GUIDELINES

As this workbook is a simplified form taken from *Journaling for Joy* just to get you started and spark your interest in beginning your inner journey, it is recommended that you:

1. Do one exercise at a time. Use as many additional pages as you feel you need to answer any of the questions found in the workbook.

2. As you do the exercises, jot down topics for future writing you want

to do, journaling questions you want to ask yourself, and results you want to achieve through you own writing.

3. Whenever possible, set aside uninterrupted time for journaling in a space that is free from distractions, so you can really be with yourself.

4. Date your writing. A date positions each piece of your writing in its proper context and demonstrates the evolution of your thoughts and feelings.

5. Give your writing a title, whenever appropriate.

6. Read over everything after your write it. Ask yourself what is the feeling tone in my writing? What does this piece say to me? What conclusions can I draw from this writing? What action or further writing needs to take place? Adding your interpretation of the significance of the events that you record will bring clarity, insights, and richness into your life. Always end each writing with a feedback statement that summarizes your response to your work as you now see it.

7. Although the exercises are taken directly from *Journaling for Joy*, it is recommended that the book be a part of your journey. It is filled with writing samples of fellow journalers to inspire and, perhaps, touch you with personal glimpses into a shared reality. These writings can serve as a travel guide to prepare the pathway for your journey.

RESULTS YOU CAN ACHIEVE THROUGH JOURNALING

- To know who you are.
- To turn problems into opportunities, gifts.
- To learn to trust yourself as your own counselor.
- To release feelings, turmoil, stress.
- To access information from your subconscious mind.
- To find answers to what seems to be unanswerable.
- To capture the teachings of your past.
- To record experiences and thoughts you want to keep and remember.
- To awaken the writer's voice within you.

- To communicate with others when talking is difficult or impossible.
- To integrate what you are learning from a class, lecture or life situation.
- To know yourself as a spiritual being.
- To heal the past.
- To live from being awake and aware of the present.
- To create the future by conscious choice.
- To understand the connection between thought and health.
- To understand your "partners" in life.
- TO CAPTURE THE JOY!

By now you are excited about getting to know who you are! Journaling is about your self-expression. It invites you to discover your truth and identify your natural skills, talents, abilities, and insights. It welcomes you to discover the answer to the basic question, "Why are you here?" Through the act of writing things down, you allow yourself to wake up, be aware, and pay attention to what your life has to teach you.

CHAPTER

Discovering Your Truth

Do you know that what you need to be happy, you already have? It will emerge from within when invited and given the chance. The exercises in chapter 1 are an invitation. It is the beginning of the journey back to your natural self—the self that is alive, full of joy, laughter, health, and creativity.

You will begin to remember that self as you write in your journal. Your thoughts will serve as a reminder, as a way back on the road to what you love. You do know what it is that you love, that which brings you joy, a sense of accomplishment, a sense of achievement. You may simply have lost track of it. Your writing will allow you to take the time to reconnect with the source of your inner knowing. Rest assured that your inner self holds nothing but the highest truth and good in store for you.

As a human being you are a precious resource containing everything you need to make your life exactly the way you want it. The seeds of the gifts you have to give are all there waiting to be nurtured. In this first chapter you will begin to open up the gifts you have to give to yourself and the world around you. You will start to discover your truth and identify your natural skills, talents, abilities, and insights.

You may be surprised by your insights as you journal to find your in-depth answers and reread those answers to write your feedback statements. It is inevitable that when you record your experience without editing, breakthroughs come. You will become aware of where you are and what changes you need to make to bring you back to yourself and *your* truth—not somebody else's idea of who you should be and what you should do.

You will learn immensely from your writing over time. By keeping a daily record you will remain in constant dialogue with your life. You will have an opportunity to question, "If this is my life, do I like it? Do I want to change it?" You will start to take more responsibility for what happens in your life.

Through logging you will notice patterns and see relationships between thoughts, feelings, and actions. By becoming the observer, you then become the planner, the designer, the critiquer, and the organizer of your life. You will learn that there is a way to live life from choice rather than reaction. There is always a way to take the driver's seat in life.

Somewhere inside of you is that great feeling of knowing that you were meant to experience peace, joy, and happiness as your natural birthright. The writing exercises in this chapter and in the chapters that follow, will help you listen to your inner voice and retrieve that natural state of being.

Easter
4/12/98

How do I feel right now about journaling writing?

I am not all that enthusiastic about it. It strikes me as being self-absorbed; however many consider it an enlightening growth process so I'm giving it a try.

What would I like journaling to do for me?

I'm not sure at this point. Perhaps I need a sounding board or a mechanism for brainstorming so that I won't bombard the people I love with remarks that they take too personally as criticisms or insults. Perhaps I just need to concretize my ideas in a non judgemental format.

Chapter 1

Here is my feedback statement that sums up what I learned and what my next step is.

Writing does seem to focus and crystalize my thoughts — to pull fragments together and to elicit ideas that I did not even realize were lurking beneath the surface — to sort of jumpstart my subconscious as it were... I guess I'll keep writing and see what unfolds...

A DAILY RECORD TO CAPTURE THE MEANING OF YOUR LIFE

When you keep a log of your experiences and read it over, weeks, months, or even years later, your writing may provide a treasured record of fond memories. Appreciation of our learning and our joy is inherent in each day's experience. It is brought out by the power of *directed intention* when we keep a written record of our events, feelings, thoughts, and what it all means. A good starting point for beginning to keep a daily record is to sit down at the end of your day, picture the day's events, and review your day. The following exercise questions are designed as a guide to help you in formulating your own daily record. Close your eyes and review your day. When you feel ready, open your eyes and respond to the following questions.

What was my first thought of the morning?

_____

_____

_____

_____

_____

How did my body feel?

_____

_____

_____

_____

What was my first movement of the day?

_____

_____

_____

_____

_____

What was the first thing I did?

_____

_____

_____

_____

_____

What did I look forward to?

_____

_____

_____

_____

_____

What did I dread?

_____

_____

_____

_____

_____

What would an objective outside observer think, watching my movements?

_____

_____

_____

_____

_____

What might not appear obvious to an observer, being known only to me?

_____

_____

_____

_____

_____

What interactions did I have with other people?

1. _____
2. _____
3. _____
4. _____
5. _____

Where did I go?

_____

_____

_____

_____

_____

What were my thoughts?

_____

_____

_____

_____

_____

_____

What happened next?

_____

_____

_____

_____

_____

What were the feelings I felt?

1. _____

2. _____

3. _____

4. _____

5. _____

What did I notice about my body?

_____

_____

_____

_____

_____

This is a description of who I was today.

_____

_____

_____

_____

_____

What is it like to be living my life today?

_____

_____

_____

_____

What was my life about today?

_____

_____

_____

_____

Here is a description of my day, adding feelings, colors, sounds, and sights:

_____

_____

_____

_____

_____

_____

_____

_____

What occurred today that wants to be remembered?

1. _____

2. _____

3. _____

4. _____

5. _____

What occurred today that needs to be resolved?

1. _____

2. _____

3. _____

4. _____

5. _____

In rereading what I have written in answer to all the questions, what does it say to me?

_____

_____

_____

_____

_____

What conclusions can I draw?

_____

_____

_____

_____

_____

_____

What action is suggested?

_____

_____

_____

_____

KEEPING A LOG FOR EVERY OCCASION

One of the simplest ways to observe yourself is by keeping a log, or simple list recording the details you're interested in knowing more about. The following exercise questions are designed to allow you to be more aware of yourself, thereby beginning the self-discovery process.

What am I dissatisfied with?

1. _____

2. _____

3. _____

4. _____

5. _____

What do I feel unfulfilled about?

1. _____

2. _____

3. _____

4. _____

5. _____

What areas would I like to assume more control over?

1. _____

2. _____

3. _____

4. _____

5. _____

What feelings or experiences do I want to increase in my life?

1. _____

2. _____

3. _____

4. _____

5. _____

If I could take a souvenir or memento from today, what would it be?

_____

_____

_____

_____

In rereading what I have written, this is what it says to me:

_____

_____

_____

_____

What conclusions can I draw?

_____

_____

_____

_____

What action is suggested?

_____

_____

_____

_____

_____

Here is a list of what I would like to say to the people who entered my life in some form today:

1. _____

_____

2. _____

_____

3. _____

_____

4. _____

_____

5. _____

_____

6. _____

_____

7. _____

_____

8. _____

_____

9. _____

_____

10. _____

_____

Here is a log of my negative thoughts and words for a day:

_____

_____

_____

_____

_____

_____

_____

_____

_____

_____

_____

_____

_____

_____

What can I learn from what I have observed?

_____

_____

_____

_____

Here is a log of my accomplishments for a week:

_____

_____

_____

_____

_____

_____

_____

_____

_____

When I look back over my accomplishments for the week, what can I learn from what I have written?

_____

_____

_____

_____

Here is a log of my frustrations during a day:

_____

_____

_____

_____

_____

_____

_____

_____

When I look back over my frustrations during a day, what can I learn from what I have written?

_____

_____

_____

_____

Here is a log of my communications for a day:

_____
_____
_____
_____
_____
_____
_____
_____
_____

As I look back over my communications for a day, what can I learn from what I have written?

_____
_____
_____
_____

What's bugging me today?

1. _____
2. _____
3. _____
4. _____
5. _____
6. _____
7. _____
8. _____
9. _____
10. _____

As I reread what's been bugging me, what conclusions can I draw?

_____

_____

_____

_____

_____

What recommendations can I make for myself?

_____

_____

_____

_____

_____

Here is a record of my loving encounters for one day:

_____

_____

_____

_____

_____

_____

_____

_____

_____

_____

_____

_____

_____

What message comes through my writing?

_____

_____

_____

_____

In my communications today, in what ways did I say what I truly felt, wanted, or needed?

1. _____

_____

2. _____

_____

3. _____

_____

4. _____

_____

5. _____

_____

After rereading the above two questions, what can I learn from what I have observed?

_____

_____

_____

_____

What thoughts and interactions did I have today that raised my self-esteem?

1. _____

_____

2. _____

_____

3. _____

_____

4. _____

_____

5. _____

_____

What thoughts and interactions did I have today that lowered my self-esteem?

1. _____

_____

2. _____

_____

3. _____

_____

4. _____

_____

5. _____

_____

In rereading my answers to these two questions, what is the learning there?

_____

_____

_____

_____

_____

_____

What was my state of energy today, from moment to moment?

_____

_____

_____

_____

_____

_____

_____

_____

_____

What do these observations about my energy level suggest to me?

_____

_____

_____

_____

Here is a log of my feelings for a day:

_____

_____

_____

_____

_____

_____

_____

_____

_____

_____

_____

_____

_____

_____

_____

In rereading my feelings for a day, what do I conclude?

_____

_____

_____

_____

Is there a feeling I wish to increase in my life? What is it?

_____

_____

_____

_____

Here is a log of the times that I experienced this feeling:

_____

_____

_____

_____

_____

_____

_____

_____

_____

_____

_____

_____

_____

_____

_____

What is my learning about the feeling I wish to increase in my life?

_____

_____

_____

_____

_____

Here is a log of what I would like to be able to erase from my day:

_____

_____

_____

_____

_____

Here is a log of my successes today:

_____

_____

_____

_____

_____

What conclusions can I draw from the answers to these two questions?

_____

_____

_____

_____

_____

Here is a log of my thoughts over a period of 15 minutes without any interference (away from all distractions and noise):

_____

_____

_____

_____

_____

_____

_____

_____

_____

_____

_____

_____

_____

_____

_____

_____

_____

_____

What does my "mind chatter" tell me about the patterns in my thinking?

_____

_____

_____ _____

_____

_____

——————————————————— ✳ ———————————————————

When your daily journaling is used as a learning experience, it becomes much more than a useless, somewhat compulsive ritual. It's a small but very critical step to reread a journaling piece and draw out the learning from it. In journaling, when you become aware of the decisions you have made and are about to make, there is a fascinating side-effect: you begin to act out of this new awareness and you become the director and designer of your life.

CHAPTER

Opening Your
Album of Memories

You ARE THE ACCUMULATION OF WHAT HAS GONE ON BEFORE YOU, AND YOUR PAST UNFOLDS endless new revelations to teach you about your present. The exercises in this chapter will help you to open up the 'album of memories' and begin forming the pictures into words.

As you start to answer the questions, you will discover that your memories are the very window to your soul. Not only can you recreate a precious and joyful memory that you will love rereading from time to time, you can also gain a new perspective on the person you have become and why.

Throughout this chapter, as you rethink and retell your story, you will retrieve the details stashed away in your memory bank and open up a treasure chest of related recollections and learning. These details will reveal important information and truths necessary to your personal healing and discover more joy.

As you journal, you will learn how to critique yourself as if you were a totally objective observer. Through this method you will gain greater insight into what you need more of in your life today so that you can live the life you want to be living. As you learn to draw on the strength of powerful and positive memories, you will gain the ability to make life-affirming choices, particularly the ones that bring you joy.

Writing about your past will open up the powerful lessons your life can teach you. Your life will become your lesson plan as you record the significant moments and experiences in writing, remember the learning of the moment, and keep a running record of your experiences. Your learning will be integrated into your life each day. By being a faithful observer, you will learn how to have the freedom to make the choices that will change your life for the better.

YOUR STORY

Recording a memory is an excellent way of opening up the window into journaling about your personal history. Even though you may think that your whole past is just a blur, as you start to write the answers to the following exercise questions, you will discover that your memories are the very window to your soul.

What's buried in my memory that would be enjoyable to recall and could tell me something about my past?

_____

_____

_____

_____

_____

_____

_____

_____

_____

_____

_____

What conclusions can I draw about this past joyful memory?

_____

_____

_____

_____

What shared experience with my best childhood friend can I remember?

_____

_____

_____

_____

_____

_____

What conclusions can I draw about this shared experience?

_____

_____

_____

_____

Here is a paragraph about a past experience I had, written in the third person as though I were writing about someone else:

_____

_____

_____

_____

_____

_____

Here is the same past experience written in the first person:

_____

_____

_____

_____

_____

_____

_____

What changes in feelings did this shift in writing bring about?

_____

_____

_____

_____

What lesson can I learn from this past experience?

_____

_____

_____

_____

What incident from my past caused me anger and why?

_____

_____

_____

_____

_____

_____

What does this incident say to me?

_____

_____

_____

_____

What conclusions can I draw?

_____

_____

_____

_____

What action, if any, is suggested?

_____

_____

_____

_____

What incident from my past caused me heartbreak and why?

_____

_____

_____

_____

_____

_____

_____

_____

What does this incident say to me?

_____

_____

_____

_____

What conclusions can I draw?

_____

_____

_____

_____

What action, if any, is suggested?

_____

_____

_____

_____

What incident in my life caused me frustration and why?

_____

_____

_____

_____

_____

_____

_____

_____

What does this incident say to me?

_____

_____

_____

_____

What conclusions can I draw?

_____

_____

_____

_____

What action, if any, is suggested?

_____

_____

_____

_____

What was an incident in my life in which I felt afraid?

_____

_____

_____

_____

_____

_____

_____

_____

What does this incident say to me?

_____

_____

_____

_____

What conclusions can I draw?

_____

_____

_____

_____

What action, if any, is suggested?

_____

_____

_____

_____

What incident in my life caused me embarrassment or shame and why?

_____

_____

_____

_____

_____

_____

_____

_____

_____

What does this incident say to me?

_____

_____

_____

_____

What conclusions can I draw?

_____

_____

_____

_____

What action, if any, is suggested?

_____

_____

_____

_____

TURNING POINTS IN YOUR LIFE

The major life decisions you made at significant moments in your past are still in effect, often subconsciously, today. We may not even have been aware that we made such a decision at the time, although we are continuing to live by it today. As you reflect on your past experience and answer the following exercise questions about the critical incidents, you may find that you are suddenly aware of the impact certain decisions and choices made on your life.

What old attitudes and decisions have I lived my life by?

1. _____

_____

2. _____

_____

3. _____

_____

4. _____

_____

5. _____

_____

6. _____

_____

7. _____

_____

8. _____

_____

9. _____

_____

10. _____

_____

What choices could I make now that will change my life for the better?

1. _____

_____

2. _____

_____

3. _____

_____

4. _____

_____

5. _____
_____

6. _____
_____

7. _____
_____

8. _____
_____

9. _____
_____

10. _____
_____

Here is a list of 10 decisions I made in my life that stand out in my memory:

1. _____
_____
_____

2. _____
_____
_____

3. _____
_____
_____

4. _____
_____
_____

5. _____
_____
_____

6. _____

_____

_____

7. _____

_____

_____

8. _____

_____

_____

9. _____

_____

_____

10. _____

_____

_____

What conclusion did I draw from each decision when it happened?

1. _____

_____

_____

2. _____

_____

_____

3. _____

_____

_____

4. _____

_____

_____

5. _____

_____

_____

6. _____

_____

_____

7. _____

_____

_____

8. _____

_____

_____

9. _____

_____

_____

10. _____

_____

_____

How has the conclusion affected my life?

1. _____

_____

_____

2. _____

_____

_____

3. _____

_____

_____

4. _____

_____

_____

5. _____

_____

_____

6. _____

_____

_____

7. _____

_____

_____

8. _____

_____

_____

9. _____

_____

_____

10. _____

_____

_____

Is it still a valid conclusion to keep today?

1. _____

_____

2. _____

_____

3. _____

_____

4. _____

_____

5. _____

_____

6. _____

_____

7. _____

_____

8. _____

_____

9. _____

_____

10._____

_____

Here is a summary about my learning from the exercise on each past decision:

1. _____

_____

_____

2. _____

_____

_____

3. _____

_____

_____

4. _____

_____

_____

5. _____

_____

_____

6. _____

_____

_____

7. _____

_____

_____

8. _____

_____

_____

9. _____

_____

_____

10. _____

_____

_____

UNDERSTANDING THE PRESENT BY REMEMBERING THE PAST

Rather than continuing to linger over past choices and regrets, you can resolve them in the present by journaling. These exercise questions are designed to give you the opportunity to understand what was "missing" and bring it back into your life through writing.

What talent did I have as a child that I would like to have developed but never did?

_____

_____

_____

Why have I never developed that talent?

_____

_____

_____

_____

_____

Do I lack confidence in this area? If yes, why? If not, why not?

_____

_____

_____

_____

_____

What have I limited myself from experiencing?

_____

_____

_____

_____

What was "missing" in my past?

_____

_____

_____

_____

What do I need to do to recover my confidence?

_____

_____

_____   _____

_____

In what areas can I express myself more fully now?

_____

_____

_____

_____

How can I use this talent now?

_____

_____

_____

_____

THE MANY DIMENSIONS SHAPING MY STORY

If we look at life through a porthole only wide enough to see what has gone wrong, our life will be a lot different than if we walk right out into the deck. If we focus on a single subject, we can get a clear picture of that one subject. But if we add a wide-angle lens, we can view a much broader picture. The whole picture is who we are. Why limit our self-perspective to a narrow focus? These exercise questions will aid you in broadening your view so that you can benefit from every aspect of your experience.

As a small child what would my kindergarten teacher say about me?

_____

_____

_____

_____

_____

_____

_____

_____

_____

As a small child what would my grandfather say about me?

_____

_____

_____

_____

_____

_____

_____

_____

As a small child what would my grandmother say about me?

_____

_____

_____

_____

_____

_____

_____

As a small child what would my mother say about me?

_____

_____

_____

_____

_____

_____

_____

As a small child what would my father say about me?

_____

_____

_____

_____

_____

_____

_____

As a small child, if I had a sibling, what would she/he say about me?

_____

_____

_____

_____

_____

_____

_____

_____

_____

As a small child what would one of my aunts have said about me?

_____

_____

_____

_____

As a small child what would one of my uncles have said about me?

_____

_____

_____

_____

As a small child what would my neighbor have said about me?

_____

_____

_____

_____

What do the answers to these questions say to me?

_____

_____

_____

_____

What conclusions can I draw?

_____
_____
_____
_____
_____

When I was a child, whose primary influence shaped me?

1. _____
2. _____
3. _____
4. _____
5. _____

In what way did their primary influence shape me?

1. _____
_____
_____

2. _____
_____
_____

3. _____
_____
_____

4. _____
_____
_____

5. _____

_____

_____

What do these primary influences say to me?

1. _____

_____

_____

2. _____

_____

_____

3. _____

_____

_____

4. _____

_____

_____

5. _____

_____

_____

What conclusions can I draw?

_____

_____

_____

_____

_____

Here is an early memory about one person who participated in my childhood that stands out in my mind:

_____

_____

_____

_____

_____

_____

_____

_____

_____

What is the learning from this early memory?

_____

_____

_____

_____

_____

Here is a paragraph about a time in my past when I was experiencing the feelings I want to have more of now:

_____

_____

_____

_____

_____

_____

_____

_____

What does this time in my past say to me?

_____

_____

_____

_____

_____

What conclusions can I draw?

_____

_____

_____

_____

What action, if any, is suggested?

_____

_____

_____

_____

_____

Life is a great adventure. By opening up the album of stored memories, you allow yourself to recreate, rethink, and recapture the valuable thoughts and precious feelings you may have missed somewhere along the way.

CHAPTER

Getting to Know Yourself:
Taking Inventory

Iᴛ's ᴏꜰᴛᴇɴ ʜᴀʀᴅ ᴛᴏ ᴊᴏᴜʀɴᴀʟ ᴍᴇᴀɴɪɴɢꜰᴜʟʟʏ ᴜɴʟᴇss ʏᴏᴜ ᴅᴜᴍᴘ ᴏᴜᴛ ᴛʜᴇ ᴅɪsᴀʀʀᴀʏ ɪɴsɪᴅᴇ your mind and get everything out where you can see it. Then you can tell what you have, and maybe put the items back in organized positions, so you can get at them more easily next time. Writing a list to "dump out" your disorder places the multitude of ideas, concerns, solutions, and action steps where you can sort them and make use of them. Order and action often come from the concrete process of writing them down.

The exercises in chapter 3 model many ways of using lists. For example, lists are an extremely valuable tool for organizing large amounts of scattered information into orderly, manageable batches—thus freeing the mind to focus at any one point. Lists are great for identifying patterns in your life, too and they often point out the way toward needed action.

A compiled list can tell us many things. A list of what experiences and conditions bring you satisfaction and joy will give you the information you need to make your moment-to-moment and major life decisions. Your life decisions can then be based on what you are best at, what is natural for you, what feels good to you, and on what you really want in life. Writing a "What I Want" list can set your desires into motion. A person who identifies what they want and is willing to commit to the action to get it, is also one who is reaching for their full potential.

Exercises in this chapter will help you to identify how you arrived where you are now and how you can get to where you want to go. Through a journal exercise in which you list the milestones in your life, you identify with the stages you have gone through to get where you are, the progressions you have made, your learnings, important decisions, inspirations, wishes and dreams, successes, and failures. This type of list will clarify which issues you have been dealing with most of your life.

Chapter 3 will guide you to become clearer about what you believe. Exercises will help you clarify your beliefs by identifying them, questioning them, perhaps changing them, refining them, and finally reaffirming them. Defining and redefining our beliefs awakens the sleeping giant inside, because our beliefs are what give us the power to act accordingly. When you become clear about your beliefs, you are more congruent and live each day with passion.

Making a list is a first—and essential step. It plants the seed and the subsequent action follows it through. As you work the journaling exercises in this chapter, you may want to "make a list" of other ideas and future journal writing topics that pop into your head. A list can always lead you to your next journaling step or assignment.

Here is my "to do" list to help me free up my energy:

1. _____

2. _____

3. _____

4. _____

5. _____

6. _____

7. _____

8. _____

9. _____

10. _____

What specific dates do I wish to have each item on my "to do" list completed?

1. _____

2. _____

3. _____

4. _____

5. _____

6. _____

7. _____

8. _____

9. _____

10. _____

How will I accomplish this?

1. _____
_____

2. _____
_____

3. _____
_____

4. _____
_____

5. _____
_____

6. _____
_____

7. _____
_____

8. _____
_____

9. _____

_____

10. _____

_____

WHAT BRINGS YOU JOY?

Joy, our desired state, is also our natural state. But a lot of confusion and interference can get between us and our natural state of joy. The following exercises are designed to enable you to walk around under a rainbow instead of walking around under a dark cloud of doom.

What brings me joy?

1. _____

2. _____

3. _____

4. _____

5. _____

6. _____

7. _____

8. _____

9. _____

10. _____

What am I best at?

1. _____

2. _____

3. _____

4. _____

5. _____

6. _____

7. _____

8. _____

9. _____

10. _____

What do I love to do?

1. _____

2. _____

3. _____

4. _____

5. _____

6. _____

7. _____

8. _____

9. _____

10. _____

What experiences give me satisfaction?

1. _____

2. _____

3. _____

4. _____

5. _____

6. _____

7. _____

8. _____

9. _____

10. _____

What do the answers to these questions have to tell me?

_____

_____

_____

What conclusions can I draw?

_____

_____

_____

_____

_____

_____

_____

What action, if any, is suggested?

_____

_____

_____

_____

_____

_____

_____

WHO ARE YOU?

How very important it is to know who we are! These exercises will enable you to contemplate who you are and delve into this important subject.

Here are seven lists (one for each day of this week) titled WHO AM I? with 10 ways of defining yourself and explaining yourself for each day.

Day One: Who Am I?

1. _____
2. _____
3. _____
4. _____
5. _____
6. _____
7. _____
8. _____
9. _____
10. _____

What have I learned about myself today?

_____
_____
_____

Day Two: Who Am I?

1. _____
2. _____
3. _____
4. _____
5. _____
6. _____
7. _____
8. _____
9. _____
10. _____

What have I learned about myself today?

_____

_____

_____

Day Three: Who Am I?

1. _____
2. _____
3. _____
4. _____
5. _____
6. _____
7. _____
8. _____
9. _____
10. _____

What have I learned about myself today?

_____

_____

_____

Day Four: Who Am I?

1. _____
2. _____
3. _____
4. _____
5. _____

6. _____

7. _____

8. _____

9. _____

10. _____

What have I learned about myself today?

_____

_____

_____

Day Five: Who Am I?

1. _____

2. _____

3. _____

4. _____

5. _____

6. _____

7. _____

8. _____

9. _____

10. _____

What have I learned about myself today?

_____

_____

_____

_____

Day Six: Who Am I?

1. _____
2. _____
3. _____
4. _____
5. _____
6. _____
7. _____
8. _____
9. _____
10. _____

What have I learned about myself today?

_____
_____
_____

Day Seven: Who Am I?

1. _____
2. _____
3. _____
4. _____
5. _____
6. _____
7. _____
8. _____
9. _____
10. _____

What have I learned about myself today?

_____

_____

_____

_____

Is there an unfolding self-portrait for this week that I can see?

_____

_____

_____

_____

Who do I want to be?

1. _____
2. _____
3. _____
4. _____
5. _____
6. _____
7. _____
8. _____
9. _____
10. _____

How do my "Who Am I" lists compare with my "Who Do I Want to Be" list?

_____

_____

_____

What action or changes do they suggest?

_____

_____

_____

_____

WHAT YOU WANT

There is a power in knowing your own mind. Every area of our lives is affected by knowing intimately what we want. The following exercise questions can set your desires into motion.

Here is my "What I Want" list without editing, ranking, or prioritizing:

1. _____

2. _____

3. _____

4. _____

5. _____

6. _____

7. _____

8. _____

9. _____

10. _____

What does my "What I Want List" have to say to me?

_____

_____

_____

_____

What actions can I take to get what I want?

1. _____

_____

2. _____

_____

3. _____

_____

4. _____

_____

5. _____

_____

6. _____

_____

7. _____

_____

8. _____

_____

9. _____

_____

10. _____

_____

Here is my "What I Don't Want" list without editing, ranking, or prioritizing:

1. _____

2. _____

3. _____

4. _____

5. _____

6. _____

7. _____

8. _____

9. _____

10. _____

What does my "What I Don't Want List" have to say to me?

_____

_____

_____

What actions am I going to take to change what I don't want?

1. _____

_____

2. _____

_____

3. _____

_____

4. _____

_____

5. _____

_____

6. _____

_____

7. _____

_____

8. _____

_____

9. _____

_____

10. _____

_____

What conclusions can I draw from my "I Want" list and my "I Don't Want" list?

_____

_____

_____

_____

MILESTONES IN YOUR LIFE

Milestones are turning points or significant events that mark and change your life. The following exercises will enable you to gain an overall perspective on your life.

Here is a list of milestones in my life so far:

1. _____

_____

2. _____

_____

3. _____

_____

4. _____

_____

5. _____

_____

6. _____

_____

7. _____

_____

8. _____

_____

9. _____

_____

10. _____

_____

What was the decision I made from each milestone about myself?

1. _____

_____

2. _____

_____

3. _____

_____

4. _____

_____

5. _____

_____

6. _____

_____

7. _____

_____

8. _____

_____

9. _____

_____

10. _____

_____

What was the decision I made about each milestone about others?

1. _____
   _____

2. _____
   _____

3. _____
   _____

4. _____
   _____

5. _____
   _____

6. _____
   _____

7. _____
   _____

8. _____
   _____

9. _____
   _____

10. _____
   _____

What decision did I make from each milestone about the way the world is?

1. _____
   _____

2. _____
   _____

3. _____
   _____

4. _____

_____

5. _____

_____

6. _____

_____

7. _____

_____

8. _____

_____

9. _____

_____

10. _____

_____

What did I learn out of these experiences?

_____

_____

_____

_____

What stages can I identify in each milestone?

1. _____

_____

2. _____

_____

3. _____

_____

4. _____

_____

5. _____

_____

6. _____

_____

7. _____

_____

8. _____

_____

9. _____

_____

10. _____

_____

What progressions can I identify from these milestones?

1. _____

_____

2. _____

_____

3. _____

_____

4. _____

_____

5. _____

_____

6. _____

_____

7. _____

_____

8. _____

_____

9. _____

_____

10. _____

_____

What decisions can I identify from these milestones?

1. _____

_____

2. _____

_____

3. _____

_____

4. _____

_____

5. _____

_____

6. _____

_____

7. _____

_____

8. _____

_____

9. _____

_____

10. _____

_____

What inspirations can I identify from each milestone?

1. _____

_____

2. _____

_____

3. _____

_____

4. _____

_____

5. _____

_____

6. _____

_____

7. _____

_____

8. _____

_____

9. _____

_____

10. _____

_____

What wishes and dreams can I identify from each milestone?

1. _____

_____

2. _____

_____

3. _____

_____

4. _____

_____

5. _____

_____

6. _____

_____

7. _____

_____

8. _____

_____

9. _____

_____

10. _____

_____

What successes can I identify from each milestone?

1. _____

_____

2. _____

_____

3. _____

_____

4. _____

_____

5. _____

_____

6. _____

_____

7. _____

_____

8. _____

_____

9. _____

_____

10. _____

_____

What failures can I identify from each milestone?

1. _____

_____

2. _____

_____

3. _____

_____

4. _____

_____

5. _____

_____

6. _____

_____

7. _____

_____

8. _____

_____

9. _____

_____

10. _____

_____

What conclusions can I draw from the writings concerning these milestones?

_____

_____

_____

Here is a list of milestones in the development of my self-esteem.

1. _____
2. _____
3. _____
4. _____
5. _____
6. _____
7. _____
8. _____
9. _____
10. _____

What conclusions can I draw from the development of my self-esteem?

_____

_____

_____

Here is a list of milestones in the declaration of my independence:

1. _____
2. _____
3. _____
4. _____
5. _____
6. _____
7. _____
8. _____
9. _____
10. _____

What conclusions can I draw in the declaration of my independence?

_____

_____

_____

YOUR BELIEFS

By examining your belief system you start to identify what your beliefs about every aspect of your life really are. The examination of your beliefs brings the awareness to change. Only by being clear about your current beliefs can you live your life from choice. Out of the following exercises an abundance of stored information from which to examine your beliefs will unfold. Don't forget to reread your answers and give yourself feedback in the space provided.

What do I believe about my family?

1. _____
2. _____
3. _____

4. _____

5. _____

_____

_____

_____

What do I believe about my friendships?

1. _____

2. _____

3. _____

4. _____

5. _____

_____

_____

_____

_____

What do I believe about my health?

1. _____

2. _____

3. _____

4. _____

5. _____

_____

_____

_____

_____

What do I believe about relationships?

1. _____
2. _____
3. _____
4. _____
5. _____

_____

_____

_____

_____

What do I believe about money?

1. _____
2. _____
3. _____
4. _____
5. _____

_____

_____

_____

_____

What do I believe about God or my higher power?

1. _____
2. _____
3. _____
4. _____
5. _____

_____

_____

_____

What do I believe about how I got here?

1. _____

2. _____

3. _____

4. _____

5. _____

_____

_____

_____

What do I believe about right and wrong?

1. _____

2. _____

3. _____

4. _____

5. _____

_____

_____

_____

What do I believe is important in life?

1. _____

2. _____

3. _____

4. _____

5. _____

_____

_____

_____

What is my purpose in life?

_____

_____

_____

_____

_____

_____

_____

_____

What do I believe about commitment?

1. _____

2. _____

3. _____

4. _____

5. _____

_____

_____

_____

_____

What do I believe about growing old?

1. _____

2. _____

3. _____

4. _____

5. _____

_____

_____

_____

What do I believe about death?

1. _____

2. _____

3. _____

4. _____

5. _____

_____

_____

_____

Here is a list of 10 beliefs I have and the significant life events that have influenced and formed each one of them:

1. _____

_____

_____

2. _____

_____

_____

3. _____

_____

_____

4. _____

_____

_____

5. _____

_____

_____

6. _____

_____

_____

7. _____

_____

_____

8. _____

_____

_____

9. _____

_____

_____

10. _____

_____

_____

What conclusions can I draw from this list?

_____

_____

_____

RECOGNIZING BLOCKS AND PATTERNS

Lists are one of the easiest ways to uncover our blocks and patterns. Lists can lead us to choosing new patterns of thinking and behaving when we don't like what we see and recognize that the old way is no longer working for us. Whatever is blocking you from getting what you want can provide the clue for making a list.

What is it that I am not getting but want to have?

1. _____
2. _____
3. _____
4. _____
5. _____
6. _____
7. _____
8. _____
9. _____
10. _____

What stands in my way of getting these things that I want?

1. _____
2. _____
3. _____
4. _____
5. _____
6. _____
7. _____
8. _____
9. _____
10. _____

What conclusions can I draw from these two lists?

_____

_____

_____

_____

Here is a list of ways I can successfully change my pattern to get what I want:

1. _____
2. _____
3. _____
4. _____
5. _____
6. _____
7. _____
8. _____
9. _____
10. _____

What seems to be blocking me from being the person I want to be?

1. _____
2. _____
3. _____
4. _____
5. _____
6. _____
7. _____
8. _____
9. _____
10. _____

What conclusions can I draw from these two lists?

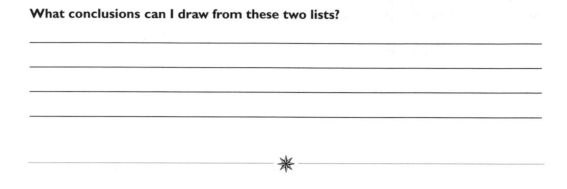

✳

Writing these types of lists is a very good way to achieve the kind of "Ah ha!" that moves you from being at "the effect" of your life to being at cause in your life events. Once you see the pattern and want to break it, you can look at your list and ask simply, "What do I need to do about this?" The list of lists you can think of to journal on is virtually endless. Here are some additional suggestions to choose from.

Things I do well.
Times I've felt fulfilled.
Things I love.
What I like about myself.
Positive experiences I've had.
People I like being with.
Ways I am like my...mother's, father's, teacher's, parent's ideal.
Excuses I sometimes use.
Times I've sold out.
Times I've been acknowledged.
Times I've been wrong, how I knew it, and what I did.
Times I've been right, how I knew it, and what I did.
Great losses in my life—and what the learning was.
Times I've been sick or had accidents—what was going on in my life at the time.
Things I would do if I were the person I admire.
Things I would do if I left my misery behind.
Things I would do if I had no excuses.
Things I need to handle in order to restore my integrity.
Times I've wanted to quit/give up.
What I want to add to my life.
What I want to eliminate from my life.
Times I've felt creative.
Things I want to be remembered for.
Dreams I am committed to realize.

CHAPTER

Writing to Create
a New Picture

WE ARE ARTISTS AND OUR CREATION IS OUR LIFE. IN CHAPTER 4 YOU WILL LEARN TO write conversations so that you can be in constant communication or dialogue with your life. A full and vital life thrives on ongoing interaction and purposeful creation. Our relationship to life can flourish with excitement and enchantment if we keep the communication with ourselves flowing and alive.

In this chapter, you will explore writing conversations that take you beyond speculating about people, events, and issues into actually being the person or event—playing out the part and speaking the lines. In writing conversations, you will discover that you really do know the other person's point of view. Even though you haven't experienced it, by discovering their voice through writing, you can access another person's reality.

You can also access *your* inner knowing through learning how to use your imagination as a channel. The dialoguing exercises presented here can connect you to your truth. Revelations can emerge that are life-changing, powerful invitations to align with your life's purpose.

Within us all is an inherent desire for peace. The exercises in this chapter will help you attain freedom from conflict and resolution of differences. You will learn how to turn a potentially damaging situation into a positive one. You will learn to recognize and change any old destructive patterns that you may still be caught up in as well as learn how to explore and pinpoint your feelings, release them, and replace them. These exercises are designed to help you climb out of the whirlpool and rise above the turmoil and mental distress so that you will get closer to living life the way you choose to live it.

You can invent countless ideas for conversations. Learn to keep your channels of conversation open. Once messages come through on a conscious level, you can deal with and act on them more effectively. When you write a dialogue, the main beneficiary is you. Instead of getting out the encyclopedia, reading another book, or seeking out someone else to advise you, first look to yourself as the authority in your life. When you write a conversation, you are really drawing from what you already know inside. You are just looking at what you know from a new and creative perspective.

Chapter 4 will be invaluable to you as you set out to create joy as your reality and main purpose now. No matter what you're going through at the moment, you have but to look for the joy, invite it to come forth, and write it into your reality.

CONVERSING WITH YOURSELF

Who knows more about you than you do? Somewhere inside of you is the answer to any question you could ever ask. In the following exercises you will tap into your answers by holding a conversation with yourself. You will have dialogues between "you, the interviewer" and "you, the interviewee." The advantage of using another person (the interviewer) is that it eliminates any self-judgment. If you don't know what one of your characters would say to the other, make it up!

Here is a conversation between my true self and me answering the question, "What does my life plan say is next for me?":

_____

_____

_____

_____

_____

_____

_____

_____

_____

_____

_____

_____

_____

_____

_____

_____

_____

What does this conversation have to say to me?

_____

_____

_____

_____

_____

What conclusions can I draw?

_____

_____

_____

_____

_____

What action, if any, is suggested?

_____

_____

_____

_____

_____

Here is a dialogue between me and the two-year old child inside of me:

_____

_____

_____

_____

_____

_____

_____

_____

_____

_____

_____

_____

_____

_____

_____

_____

_____

_____

_____

_____

_____

What does this conversation have to say to me?

_____
_____
_____
_____
_____
_____

What conclusions can I draw?

_____
_____
_____
_____
_____

What action, if any, is suggested?

_____
_____
_____
_____
_____

Here is a conversation between me and the rebellious teenager inside of me:

_____
_____
_____
_____
_____
_____

_____

_____

_____

_____

_____

_____

_____

_____

_____

_____

_____

_____

_____

_____

What does this conversation have to say to me?

_____

_____

_____

_____

_____

What conclusions can I draw?

_____

_____

_____

_____

_____

What action, if any, is suggested?

_____

_____

_____

_____

_____

Here is a conversation between the mail and female side of my personality:

_____

_____

_____

_____

_____

_____

_____

_____

_____

_____

_____

_____

_____

_____

_____

_____

_____

_____

_____

_____

What does this conversation have to say to me?

_____

_____

_____

_____

_____

What conclusions can I draw?

_____

_____

_____

_____

_____

What action, if any, is suggested?

_____

_____

_____

_____

_____

Here is a dialogue between me and my spiritual self:

_____

_____

_____

_____

_____

_____

_____

_____

_____

_____

_____

_____

_____

_____

_____

_____

_____

_____

_____

_____

What does this dialogue have to say to me?

_____

_____

_____

_____

_____

What conclusions can I draw?

_____

_____

_____

_____

What action, if any, is suggested?

_____

_____

_____

_____

_____

Here is a debate between what I really want to do versus what I am willing to do:

_____

_____

_____

_____

_____

_____

_____

_____

_____

_____

_____

_____

_____

_____

_____

_____

_____

_____

_____

What does this debate have to tell to me?

_____

_____

_____

_____

_____

What conclusions can I draw?

_____

_____

_____

_____

_____

What action, if any, is suggested?

_____

_____

_____

_____

_____

Here is a conversation between me and a part of my body that I am unsatisfied with:

_____

_____

_____

_____

_____

_____

_____

_____

_____

_____

_____

_____

_____

_____

_____

_____

_____

_____

_____

_____

_____

What does this conversation have to say to me?

_____

_____

_____

_____

What conclusions can I draw?

_____

_____

_____

_____

What action, if any, is suggested?

_____

_____

_____

_____

_____

Here is a conversation between me and a part of my body that I am satisfied with:

_____

_____

_____

_____

_____

_____

_____

_____

_____

_____

_____

_____

_____

_____

_____

_____

_____

_____

_____

What does this conversation have to say to me?

_____

_____

_____

_____

_____

_____

What conclusions can I draw?

_____

_____

_____

_____

_____

_____

What action, if any, is suggested?

_____

_____

_____

_____

_____

_____

CONVERSING WITH ANOTHER PERSON

Creating a conversation with another person can lead to resolving an inner conflict or sense of unease over a recent or long-standing difficulty. The following exercise questions can help you get a better grasp of your own position while gaining insights into someone else's point of view.

Here is a conversation between my mentor and myself regarding guidance or advice that I need about a particular problem:

_____

_____

_____

_____

_____

_____

_____

_____

_____

_____

_____

_____

_____

_____

_____

_____

_____

_____

_____

What is this conversation telling me?

_____

_____

_____

_____

_____

What conclusions can I draw?

_____

_____

_____

_____

_____

What action, if any, is suggested?

_____

_____

_____

_____

Here is a conversation between a person who has already achieved what I wish to achieve and myself:

_____

_____

_____

_____

_____

_____

_____

_____

_____

_____

_____

_____

_____

_____

_____

_____

_____

_____

What does this conversation say to me?

_____

_____

_____

_____

_____

What conclusions can I draw?

_____

_____

_____

_____

What action, if any, is suggested?

_____

_____

_____

_____

Here is a conversation between myself and another person that will help me prepare for an upcoming encounter with that person:

_____

_____

_____

_____

_____

_____

_____

_____

_____

_____

_____

_____

_____

_____

_____

_____

_____

_____

What does this conversation have to say to me?

_____

_____

_____

_____

What conclusions can I draw?

_____

_____

_____

_____

_____

What action, if any, is suggested?

_____

_____

_____

_____

_____

Here is a conversation between someone I am having a current relationship with and myself:

_____

_____

_____

_____

_____

_____

_____

_____

_____

_____

_____

_____

_____

_____

_____

_____

_____

_____

_____

_____

What does this conversation have to say to me?

_____

_____

_____

_____

_____

What conclusions can I draw?

_____

_____

_____

_____

_____

What action, if any, is suggested?

_____

_____

_____

_____

_____

Here is a conversation between myself and someone I admire:

_____

_____

_____

_____

_____

_____

_____

_____

_____

_____

_____

_____

_____

_____

_____

_____

_____

_____

_____

_____

What does this conversation have to say to me?

_____

_____

_____

_____

_____

What conclusions can I draw?

_____

_____

_____

_____

_____

What action, if any, is suggested?

_____

_____

_____

_____

CONVERSING WITH AN IDEA

Another kind of conversation that can produce very powerful results is writing a dialogue with any idea or concept that is currently affecting your life. Here are some exercises to get you started.

Here is an argument between myself and my guilt:

_____

_____

_____

_____

_____

_____

_____

_____

_____

_____

_____

_____

_____

_____

_____

_____

_____

_____

_____

_____

_____

_____

What does this argument have to say to me?

_____

_____

_____

_____

_____

What conclusions can I draw?

_____

_____

_____

_____

_____

What action, if any, is suggested?

_____

_____

_____

_____

Here is a three-way conversation between "Want, Need, and Desire" to clarify what I most want:

_____

_____

_____

_____

_____

_____

_____

_____

_____

_____

_____

_____

_____

_____

_____

What does this conversation have to say to me?

_____

_____

_____

_____

_____

What conclusions can I draw?

_____

_____

_____

_____

_____

What action, if any, is suggested?

_____

_____

_____

_____

_____

Here is a dialogue between myself and something that is missing from my life (joy, creativity, romance, success...):

_____

_____

_____

_____

_____

_____

_____

_____

_____

_____

_____

_____

_____

_____

_____

_____

_____

_____

_____

_____

What does this dialogue have to say to me?

_____

_____

_____

_____

_____

What conclusions can I draw?

_____

_____

_____

_____

_____

What action, if any, is suggested?

_____

_____

_____

_____

_____

_____

CONVERSING TO DISCOVER THE JOY

Conversations provide a most effective means to writing yourself to a chosen result. Start with the result. What do you want? What is the result you want to produce? Visualize it clearly. Put it into words. Then identify someone or something to dialogue with. Here is a short exercise to help you get started.

What is joy, for me?

_____

_____

_____

_____

_____

_____

When is the last time I can remember experiencing pure, undiluted joy?

_____

_____

_____

_____

_____

_____

Here is an imaginary conversation with "joy" itself:

_____

_____

_____

_____

_____

_____

_____

_____

_____

_____

_____

_____

_____

_____

_____

_____

_____

_____

_____

_____

What does this conversation have to say to me?

_____

_____

_____

_____

_____

What conclusions can I draw?

_____

_____

_____

_____

What action, if any, is suggested?

_____

_____

_____

_____

CONVERSING TO ACHIEVE CLARITY

When indecision or living in limbo becomes too uncomfortable, when you're spinning your wheels and not getting anywhere, when you feel pulled in different directions by conflicting intentions, it's time to get clear on what you really want. One way to start is by choosing a destination. The following exercises will enable you to focus on the outcome you intend to reach and help you eliminate the scatter.

Where do I want to go?

_____

_____

_____

_____

_____

_____

_____

_____

_____

_____

_____

_____

Here is a drawing of a road map done in bold ink, picturing a major freeway flowing straight to my chosen destination. I have pictured all the side diversions and detours, with their different destinations, in a fainter color.

What conclusions can I draw about my road map and its side diversions?

_____

_____

_____

_____

_____

Here is a heart-to-heart talk with myself or the "selves" inside of me to help me achieve the clarity I need:

_____

_____

_____

_____

_____

_____

_____

_____

_____

_____

_____

_____

_____

_____

_____

_____

_____

_____

_____

_____

_____

_____

What conclusions can I draw from this talk?

_____

_____

_____

_____

_____

Here is a dialogue between myself and a state that I would like to achieve:

_____

_____

_____

_____

_____

_____

_____

_____

_____

_____

_____

_____

_____

_____

_____

_____

_____

_____

_____

_____

_____

_____

What conclusions can I draw about this dialogue?

_____

_____

_____

_____

_____

CONVERSING TO WORK THROUGH CONFLICT

Conflict puts a person in bondage. It ties people up emotionally and restricts their energy, locking it into the dilemma of attack/defend/withdraw. This dialogue exercise will aid you in getting in touch with what is causing a conflict, what is bothering you about a relationship, and what is at the root of the pain or discomfort.

Here is a conversation between myself and someone who is repeatedly aggravating to me:

_____

_____

_____

_____

_____

_____

_____

_____

_____

_____

_____

_____

_____

_____

_____

_____

_____

_____

_____

_____

_____

_____

What conclusions can I draw from this conversation?

_____

_____

_____

_____

_____

Here is a conversation between myself and another person, saying exactly what I secretly wish I could say to him/her:

_____

_____

_____

_____

_____

_____

_____

_____

_____

_____

_____

_____

_____

_____

_____

_____

_____

_____

_____

_____

What conclusions can I draw from this conversation?

_____

_____

_____

_____

_____

CONVERSING TO RELEASE YOUR FEELINGS

Once you have identified what it is that you are feeling, you can release that feeling by writing a conversation directly with that feeling or its cause. Here are some sample exercises to help you get started.

Here is a conversation between myself and my anger or its cause:

_____

_____

_____

_____

_____

_____

_____

_____

_____

_____

_____

_____

_____

_____

_____

_____

_____

_____

_____

_____

What conclusions can I draw from this conversation?

_____

_____

_____

_____

_____

_____

Here is a conversation between myself and my sorrow:

_____

_____

_____

_____

_____

_____

_____

_____

_____

_____

_____

_____

_____

_____

_____

_____

_____

_____

_____

What conclusion can I draw from this conversation?

_____

_____

_____

_____

_____

What is my tension and stress about?

_____

_____

_____

_____

_____

Here is a conversation between stress and freedom:

_____

_____

_____

_____

_____

_____

_____

_____

_____

_____

_____

_____

_____

_____

_____

_____

What conclusions can I draw about this conversation?

_____

_____

_____

_____

_____

✳

Through the process of living your life, unlimited ideas for conversations will come to you. Get into the habit of jotting them down and taking them to your journal. Pay attention: trust and tap into your own inner wisdom, your own natural knowing. Instead of muddling around in the heaviness of any situation, you can dance with your creative potential through journal dialoguing.

CHAPTER

Exploring Your Questions,
Discovering Your Answers

QUESTIONING IS AN ACTIVITY THAT CHECKS AND RENEWS OUR SPIRIT. IN ORDER TO COME up with powerful solutions, we have to ask powerful questions. The questioning attitude presumes an attitude of openness—that we don't know it all and we're open to new dimensions of learning, experiences, and information.

Simple questions like: "What should I do today?," "What should I wear today?," and even "What should I cook today?" show that one is living in dialogue with one's life, not settled into humdrum boredom and not living with anyone else's answers.

When someone has stopped asking and answering questions, they have probably stopped growing and being vital. Creation holds suspense, mystery and the unknown. It demands inquiry and contemplation. It celebrates the questions!

In this chapter, you will learn about the "art" of questioning—a practice that is foreign to the way many people were brought up. They have been given answers, not questions, and their questions have been suppressed, not encouraged. It is so rare in homes and social groups for someone to ask us: "What do you really think?"; What do you know?"; or "What do you feel?"

The questions in chapter 5 will help you practice the art of questioning in your journal. Through learning to ask yourself in-depth questions you can reach your inner psyche where hidden feelings and motivations lie. When the question process begins, you will learn how to come to terms with whatever feelings and facts you have been avoiding. Then you can start to direct inner resources toward asking and answering the questions that lead to change and well-being.

Life offers us a continuum of questions. Chapter 5 will give you many ideas for turning your journal into a veritable hotbed for sprouting new ideas and discovering who you are. You can turn every piece of journal writing into ten new questions, and write new self-discovery pieces on each one. Questions have a way of multiplying into gardens of blossoming flowers.

The kind of exploring that chapter 5 demands marks positive movement—from vague uneasiness to the search for truth and meaning. If you're willing to commit the time and effort to both ask and answer your own questions, as well as to be your own teacher, you will find yourself within the wisdom or knowingness that brings you back to yourself and joy.

THE ART OF SELF-INVESTIGATION

In journaling, writing down the questions your life gives you provides a means of inviting your inner answers to come forward. The following exercise questions invite the creative process. It starts with not knowing and creates answers out of the void or nothingness.

What question do I need to answer for myself or what do I want to know?

_____

_____

_____

_____

_____

_____

What information can I give myself in answer to the above question?

_____

_____

_____

_____

_____

_____

_____

_____

_____

_____

_____

_____

_____

_____

What does my question and answer have to say to me?

_____

_____

_____

_____

_____

_____

What conclusions can I draw?

_____

_____

_____

_____

_____

_____

What action, if any, is suggested?

_____

_____

_____

_____

_____

Am I happy? Why or why not?

_____

_____

_____

_____

_____

_____

_____

_____

_____

_____

_____

_____

_____

_____

_____

_____

_____

_____

What does my writing about my happiness have to say to me?

_____

_____

_____

_____

_____

What conclusions can I draw?

_____

_____

_____

_____

_____

What action, if any, is suggested?

_____

_____

_____

_____

_____

Do I love the people I associate with? Why or why not?

_____

_____

_____

_____

_____

_____

What does my answer to this question have to say to me?

_____

_____

_____

_____

_____

What conclusions can I draw?

_____

_____

_____

_____

What action, if any, is suggested?

_____

_____

_____

_____

Do I love the work I am doing? Why or why not?

_____

_____

_____

_____

_____

_____

_____

_____

_____

_____

_____

_____

_____

What does the answer about the work I am doing have to say to me?

_____

_____

_____

_____

_____

What conclusions can I draw?

_____

_____

_____

_____

_____

What action, if any, is suggested?

_____

_____

_____

_____

_____

Why am I _____ **?**
(Fill in the blank with a feeling that you are currently experiencing.)

_____

_____

_____

_____

_____

_____

_____

_____

_____

_____

_____

_____

What does my writing regarding my feeling have to say to me?

_____

_____

_____

_____

_____

What conclusions can I draw?

_____

_____

_____

_____

_____

What action, if any, is suggested?

_____

_____

_____

_____

_____

What do I want?

_____

_____

_____

_____

_____

_____

_____

_____

_____

_____

_____

_____

_____

_____

What does my writing about what I want have to say to me?

_____

_____

_____

_____

_____

What conclusions can I draw?

_____

_____

_____

_____

_____

_____

What action, if any, is suggested?

_____

_____

_____

_____

_____

_____

SEARCHING FOR LOVE: QUESTIONS FROM YOUR HEART

It may take some practice to know how to ask the questions that nurture acceptance and growth. Those questions come from a place of love. They offer to listen unconditionally with a deep level of trust that you do know your own answers. In the following exercise try asking yourself a question that you would like to be answered by a person who loves and respects you (your grandparent, your parent, etc.) Cherish yourself like a nurturing grandparent in this writing, and explore the questions of your life as you write to come up with the answers:

My question:

_____

_____

_____

The discussion that ensues between myself and a person who loves and respects me regarding the above question:

_____

_____

_____

_____

_____

_____

_____

_____

_____

_____

_____

_____

_____

_____

_____

_____

_____

_____

_____

What does my writing have to say to me?

_____

_____

_____

_____

What conclusions can I draw?

_____

_____

_____

_____

_____

What action, if any, is suggested?

_____

_____

_____

_____

_____

SEARCH FOR TRUTH: QUESTIONS THAT DON'T WANT TO BE ANSWERED

People sometimes don't want to ask questions they'd rather not know the answers to. They may be forced to realize something about themselves that they'd rather not know. Fear of reprisal may stop a person from searching for the truth and it can seem better not to know. Serious questioning may be put off for years. Use this exercise as practice in the gentle art of objective self-investigation, with the sole intent of learning and knowing, not judging and making yourself wrong. You have nothing to lose and everything to gain.

What is the question I'd rather not know the answer to? (Examples: Why do I keep bailing my grown children out of trouble?; Why am I so hard on me?; What is the deal with my eating?; Why do I shop?; Why am I crazy today?; Why can't I experience intimacy in my relationships?)

_____

_____

What are my answers, suggestions to this question?

_____

_____

_____

_____

_____

_____

_____

_____

_____

_____

_____

_____

_____

_____

_____

_____

_____

_____

_____

_____

_____

What does my writing have to say to me?

_____

_____

_____

_____

_____

What conclusions can I draw?

_____

_____

_____

_____

_____

What action, if any, is suggested?

_____

_____

_____

_____

_____

WHERE ARE YOU ON YOUR PATH?

I have found this question to be an extremely valuable one. This could be one of the most important and illuminating questions you can ever ask yourself. It positions you. It gets you into the here and now. The more you ask it the more aware you become. The more aware you are, the more you can become the person you were meant to be.

Where am I in my life right now?

_____

_____

_____

_____

_____

_____

_____

_____

_____

_____

_____

_____

_____

_____

_____

_____

_____

_____

_____

_____

_____

Where do I want to be in my life right now?

_____

_____

_____

_____

_____

_____

_____

_____

_____

_____

What does this writing have to say to me?

_____

_____

_____

_____

_____

_____

What conclusions can I draw?

_____

_____

_____

_____

_____

_____

What action, if any, is suggested?

_____

_____

_____

_____

_____

_____

QUEST FOR QUESTIONS

Questions always bring up more questions. How long must this keep going on? Perhaps for the rest of your life. A shift does finally come when you have more answers than questions. The more you question, the more you know yourself. Here are some excellent exercise questions to write about:

Why don't I have time to journal?

_____

_____

_____

_____

_____

_____

_____

_____

What conclusions can I draw from my answer?

_____

_____

_____

_____

_____

How can I forgive myself or someone else?

_____

_____

_____

_____

_____

_____

_____

_____

_____

What conclusions can I draw from my answer?

_____

_____

_____

_____

_____

How can I know I am free?

_____

_____

_____

_____

_____

_____

_____

_____

_____

_____

_____

_____

_____

_____

What conclusions can I draw from my answer?

_____

_____

_____

_____

_____

How do I get where I want to go?

_____

_____

_____

_____

_____

_____

_____

_____

_____

_____

_____

What conclusions can I draw from my answer?

_____

_____

_____

_____

What part of me do I want to express?

_____

_____

_____

_____

_____

_____

_____

_____

_____

_____

What conclusions can I draw from my answer?

_____

_____

_____

_____

_____

What do I want someone to know about me?

_____

_____

_____

_____

_____

_____

_____

_____

What conclusions can I draw from my answer?

_____

_____

_____

_____

_____

What is love?

_____

_____

_____

_____

_____

_____

_____

_____

_____

What conclusions can I draw from my answer?

_____

_____

_____

_____

_____

How can I experience more love?

_____

_____

_____

_____

_____

_____

_____

_____

_____

What conclusions can I draw from my answer?

_____

_____

_____

_____

_____

_____

What do I need to communicate?

_____

_____

_____

_____

_____

_____

_____

_____

_____

_____

_____

What conclusions can I draw from my answer?

_____

_____

_____

_____

_____

What part of my life is "working?"

_____

_____

_____

_____

_____

_____

_____

What part of my life is "not working?"

_____

_____

_____

_____

_____

_____

_____

_____

What do my answers have to say to me?

_____

_____

_____

_____

What conclusions can I draw?

_____

_____

_____

_____

What action, if any, is suggested?

_____

_____

_____

_____

What makes my heart sing?

_____

_____

_____

_____

_____

_____

_____

_____

_____

_____

_____

What conclusions can I draw from my answer?

_____

_____

_____

_____

_____

What is my biggest dream?

_____

_____

_____

_____

_____

_____

_____

_____

_____

_____

_____

_____

What conclusions can I draw from my answer?

_____

_____

_____

_____

_____

_____

What can I do to give back to those who have given to me?

_____

_____

_____

_____

_____

_____

_____

_____

_____

What conclusions can I draw from my answer?

_____

_____

_____

_____

_____

What can I do to make a difference in the world?

_____

_____

_____

_____

_____

_____

_____

_____

_____

What conclusions can I draw from my answer?

_____

_____

_____

_____

_____

——————————————————— ✳ ———————————————————

Revitalization occurs by developing the art of self-investigation. Ideally your life would always be an open file. Encourage your own curiosity and keep asking questions. Within every question also lies the answer. By listening to your answers, you begin to see your life as a tapestry, and only by looking for the missing pieces can you hope to achieve a work of art.

CHAPTER

Letter Writing to Keep
Your Relationships Alive

YOU MIGHT NOT THINK OF LETTER WRITING AS HAVING A PLACE IN YOUR JOURNAL. BUT the letters you write and receive are a vital part of your life. They communicate what was important to you in a particular time and place, and what you wanted to share. Letters are sometimes the only means we have of keeping a relationship alive.

Wonderful letters nurture and connect us. They are an investment of the heart, paid off in value that accrues over time. When we use our time to write letters instead of automatically turning on the TV or picking up the telephone, we feel rejuvenated and our energy is restored.

Chapter 6 gives you permission to choose the letters you really want to write and the relationships you really want to invest greater energy in—including the relationship with yourself. By writing love letters to yourself and saving them in your journal to read again and again over the years, you can take responsibility for giving yourself the love you may have missed out on and deserve. You can take out your letters to yourself whenever you need to be supported, nurtured, and reminded of your goals.

The answers to the questions in this chapter will demonstrate the qualities that make letters special to you. Being able to write well is not the key to creating letters that touch someone's heart. You will come to realize that you don't have to be an accomplished writer to create a letter that someone will love to receive.

When you open up and express the full range of your feelings in a letter, you imbue a sense of certainty and assurance into your own evolving personal identity. One of the most valuable results of writing letters is to free up buried energy allowing you to think and feel things through. This may not lead to immediate resolution or inner peace, but it will lead to change and prepare you for the next step.

The exercises in this chapter will help you to see letter writing in an entirely new light. Writing letters can help you to be focused and clear, to see the real issues facing you, and to set healing into motion. Letters also present an opportunity to reach out and support those we care about as well as share valuable insights.

As you work chapter 6, you will begin to realize that, more often than not, letter writing turns out to be more for ourselves than anyone else. You'll probably be amazed at how much better you'll feel having put your thoughts, feelings, and concerns on paper. And, once you start to feel better, you can begin living your life from joy!

LETTER WRITING: THE ART OF CONNECTION

Your journal is a good place to list notes about what you want to communicate in future letters. When you have a list of events and ideas as they have occurred to you, you have the basic outline or content for a letter. The following exercises will aid you in using your journal as a central clearing system for your written correspondence and unify many disparate aspects of your life into one central location.

Here is a list of the people I want or need to communicate with:

1. _____

2. _____

3. _____

4. _____

5. _____

6. _____

7. _____

8. _____

9. _____

10. _____

Here is a list of events and ideas that I wish to share with the above people:

1. _____
_____
_____

2. _____
_____
_____

3. _____
_____
_____

4. _____
_____
_____

5. _____
_____
_____

6. _____
_____

7. _____
_____
_____

8. _____

_____

_____

9. _____

_____

_____

10. _____

_____

_____

Here is a love letter I can write to myself that I can read whenever I need to be supported, nurtured, and reminded of my hopes, wishes, and dreams:

LETTERS TO SAVE

Being able to write well is not the key to creating letters that touch someone's heart. Children's letters demonstrate that it is the communication of our feelings that is most meaningful. We treasure letters that overflow with shared love and connect us with the news in a personal way.

What qualities make letters special to me?

_____

_____

_____

_____

_____

What can I learn from the letters that are special to me about writing letters that someone might want to save?

_____

_____

_____

_____

_____

LETTERS FOR SPECIAL OCCASIONS

Your own creations, whether they be a letter, a picture, or a Valentine you make yourself can be infinitely more personal, poignant, beautiful, and fun than a commercially produced card. Letters enrich both yourself and others. They summarize, capsulize, and concentrate our experience. Letters document relationships. Letters are great for hellos and good-byes. Letters can mark milestones—a special birthday or graduation. This exercise to mark milestones of our growth will enable us to open up and express the full range of our feelings about them. This turns our growth into a conscious, rather than an unconscious process.

Here are three letters written to mark three separate occasions which are milestones of growth and in which I participated—either my own (turning 40, for example), a member of my family (their graduation, their baptism, first words spoken, for example), or a friend's (a wedding, a memorable act of generosity, for example):

Letter 1.

Letter 2.

Letter 3.

What do these letters reveal to me?

_____

_____

_____

_____

_____

_____

LETTERS FOR RELEASE; THE UNSENT LETTER; WISDOM LETTER

In relationships, what is left unexpressed has a tendency to preoccupy us subconsciously. Simply expressing our thoughts and feelings, even without expectation of any response, can be very therapeutic and healing. When we have difficulty communicating our needs and wants, writing a letter not intending to be sent is an excellent way to organize and clarify what we really want to say, without having to edit our thoughts to avoid hurting or offending someone. Communication blocks in relationships can also be circumvented in a thoughtfully worded letter—a letter that brings forth your own inner wisdom to unlock your feelings of love, caring, and understanding.

Here is my letter to someone I'd like to write to, simply expressing my thoughts, feelings, and concerns:

What conclusions can I draw after rereading the letter I just wrote?

_____

_____

_____

_____

_____

Here is a letter that I will never send, saying whatever I feel like saying, uncensored, right out, to someone that I'd like to write to:

What conclusion can I draw after rereading the letter I wrote?

_____

_____

_____

_____

_____

Here is a "wisdom letter" written to someone I care about who I'd like to reach out to and support with my shared wisdom:

What conclusions can I draw from this letter?

_____

_____

_____

_____

_____

LETTERS OF THANKS

Almost nothing feels as good as expressing our thanks to someone we appreciate and who has made a difference in our lives. The simplest letter can be one we'll want to save forever in our journals.

Here are three letters of thanks to three individuals who I appreciate and who have made a difference in my life:

Letter 1.

Letter 2.

Letter 3.

What conclusions can I draw from the three letters of thanks which I wrote?

_____

_____

_____ _____

_____

_____

———————————————— ✳ ————————————————

Here is your invitation to start writing letters. If you are already a letter writer, write more. Share your life with those you cherish. Letter writing is one of the highest forms of self-expression. It keeps you in touch with your thoughts and feelings, and by participating with those you love you become richer. Letter writing is a self-affirmation of the most benevolent kind.

C H A P T E R

Releasing Your Incredible
Inner Force

THE UNLIMITED POWER OF THE SUBCONSCIOUS MIND RESEMBLES THE VASTNESS OF THE heavens. Your subconscious mind knows no restrictions of time and space. Chapter 7 will teach you how to become the voyager and explore your subconscious mind.

The subconscious mind is the home of your deepest, most heart-felt desires. It does your every bidding. It asks no questions and will accept as fact whatever you consider to be true. The subconscious is limitless. It remembers everything you think, feel, say and do, and stores it quickly in perfect order to return it to you exactly as given. It is a humble, efficient servant always eager to create. It speaks in the language of pictures, symbols and images. Because the subconscious mind speaks in this language, Chapter 7 encourages the use of fantasy in journaling as a most effective means of initiating change.

Great benefits from the use of fantasy thinking were obtained by a few great inventors, composers, and mystics who were keenly aware of the power of the subconscious. Your writing in this chapter will take you on journeys into fantasy writing—one of the most direct means of tapping into unlimited intelligence (possibility thinking), as well as for reaching our potential, and experiencing our joy.

However, when you're attempting to open the window and look into your inner knowing, you can't wave a magic wand and expect everything to jump into place in a perfectly ordered picture. This kind of writing experience takes time and patience. Chapter 7 will give you some practice so that listening within becomes more and more natural. With practice your trust builds, and you find yourself more able to slip in and out of the realm of your deep inner knowing. And with time your inner knowing will reveal more and more of the magic and mystery that is inside you.

Journaling from the place of inner knowing takes you beneath surface concerns to the very heart of the matter. As you work the exercises in this chapter and explore the subconscious mind, you'll find that it contains an infinite library of universal truth. When you direct the conscious mind for guidance and information, the wisdom you seek will present itself.

OPENING TO THE POWER OF THE SUBCONSCIOUS

Astronomers use telescopes to explore the reservoirs of space and see the revelation of the stars. Journal writing is the telescope to explore the universe of our subconscious mind. The subconscious mind has the ability to tap into unlimited intelligence. This concept is called possibility thinking. A useful form of possibility thinking in journal writing is achieved through the use of fantasy. The following exercises are simple techniques to use in contacting the subconscious.

As I close my eyes I ask myself, "What information wants to come through me?" I will remain quiet and receptive for a few minutes. Then I will open my eyes and begin writing my thoughts without any editing.

_____

_____

_____

_____

_____

_____

_____

_____

_____

_____

_____

_____

_____

_____

_____

_____

_____

_____

What does my writing say to me? (I will let the feedback statement choose me. I won't think about it, I'll just let it come.)

_____

_____

_____

_____

_____

NATURE AS YOUR METAPHOR

Nature can be a rich and revealing metaphor for where we seem to be in our lives. Each aspect of nature can be our teacher when we invite forth the metaphor from our subconscious.

What in nature am I like?

_____

_____

_____

_____

_____

_____

_____

_____

_____

_____

_____

_____

_____

_____

_____

_____

_____

_____

What does my writing about what I am like in nature say to me?

_____

_____

_____

_____

_____

ACCESSING YOUR INNER WISDOM

In accessing inner wisdom, first you must trust that it is there. Wisdom is such a powerful idea. Synonyms for wisdom are knowledge, learning, and enlightenment. You have all those within you. I encourage daydreaming as a method of accessing your inner wisdom. The legacy of accessing inner wisdom is that you dip beneath the analytical surface to the deeper currents of inner truth, awareness, and enlightenment.

I will now write by using my imagination and by daydreaming in order to obtain the guidance I seek:

_____

_____

_____

_____

_____

_____

_____

_____

_____

_____

_____

_____

_____

_____

_____

_____

_____

_____

What does my writing have to say to me?

_____

_____

_____

_____

_____

ACCESSING A DREAM MESSAGE WHILE SLEEPING

Dreams can provide us with a gift of truth from the subconscious mind. If you want to unlock the puzzle of who you are, open the treasure chest of swirling internal possibilities, dreams can be one of the pathways to the magic of your life.

Here is a sequence of a dream I had, written as soon as I woke up from the dream:

_____

_____

_____

_____

_____

_____

_____

_____

_____

_____

_____

_____

_____

_____

_____

_____

_____

What were the thoughts and feelings that came up during this dream?

_____

_____

_____

_____

_____

_____

_____

_____

_____

_____

_____

_____

_____

_____

_____

_____

What is my dream saying to me?

_____

_____

_____

_____

_____

UNLEASH YOUR IMAGINATION—THE JOY OF PRETENDING

Stories, like dreams, invite us into the joy of discovering and learning. Out of the treasure of our imagination we can tap a fantasy rich in meaning and messages. Some messages are brilliantly obvious and others are hidden behind the gauze curtains of metaphor. To ignite your imagination takes nothing more than giving yourself permission to play and pretend.

I am going on a journey to:

_____

Here is a list of all the things I want to take with me on my imaginary journey (my list can be unlimited—I can even pack a nightingale or a diamond tiara):

1. _____

2. _____

3. _____

4. _____

5. _____

6. _____

7. _____

8. _____

9. _____

10. _____

What conclusions can I draw about my list of things to take with me on my imaginary journey?

_____

_____

_____

_____

_____

Here is my make believe story about my adventure (I can go anywhere, do anything, and the domain I create can bring me joy):

_____

_____

_____

_____

_____

_____

_____

_____

_____

_____

_____

_____

_____

_____

_____

_____

_____

_____

What does my fantasy have to say to me?

_____

_____

_____

_____

_____

Here is a poem titled according to my desired action or result:

_____

_____

_____

_____

_____

_____

_____

_____

_____

_____

_____

_____

_____

_____

_____

_____

_____

_____

What does this poem have to say to me?

_____

_____

_____

_____

_____

———————————————————— ✳ ————————————————————

Now that you have begun to explore your subconscious mind or your inner knowing you have learned that there is an unlimited wealth of information and resources inside that you can access any time simply by using your imagination to feed yourself the guidance you seek. By stepping out of your conscious state, you allow your subconscious inner knowing to access the symbols and imagery of universal truth.

C H A P T E R

The Magic of
Group Journaling

WRITING IN A GROUP IS MAGICAL. IT IS LIKE BEING IN AN IMPROMPTU DRAMA THAT unfolds right on the spot. People gather to develop their individual roles and plots which play themselves out in the theater of the whole. The audience is both playwright and players. Writers bring their life scripts to the group and rehearse their tragedies and fantasies on the stage.

As those in the journaling group participate, an awareness of the universality of the growth process we all share is brought to the fore. Each shared emotion sparks a tie with the thoughts, feelings, and situations of others in the group. Each person's learning becomes every person's learning.

In a group, the writer's voice in all of us comes out. One writer's work is touched and shaped by the work of others. The synergy of the group deepens the work and empowers the individual.

By answering the questions in this chapter you will learn how to start a journaling group and begin to understand how, through listening, sharing, and growing together, these group sessions can give powerful results.

STARTING YOUR OWN JOURNALING GROUP

You may find people among your friends and acquaintances, in your neighborhood, school, church, family, place of work, club, or organization who will be interested in meeting together to journal. There is no perfect number of people in a group. Six people is a good number to begin with but you can still do the work you have decided to do with just two people in a group.

The place your Journal Group meets should be private, quiet, and have enough room for people to spread out in their own cocoon of personal space.

How long your journaling group meets is up to the members and their needs but a definite, regular time for beginning and ending the Journal Group meetings should be observed. They should include a quiet time for writing followed by a sharing session.

Meetings should be exclusively for journaling. Twenty to thirty minutes is usually given for the initial writing, followed by twenty minutes of coming together to share. After twenty minutes of sharing, it is time to begin writing again.

People should always feel free to move quietly about, go to the bathroom, or get something to drink if they like. They are also free, if they choose, not to write.

To wrap up the meeting, you can take about ten minutes to write a poem, or just a sentence or two to bring closure to the journal writing experience. Five minutes for sharing this work concludes the session.

Here's a list of people I want to invite to journal:

1. _____

2. _____

3. _____

4. _____

5. _____

6. _____

7. _____

8. _____

9. _____

10. _____

Why did I pick these individuals to be in my journaling group?

1. _____

2. _____

3. _____

4. _____

5. _____

6. _____

7. _____

8. _____

9. _____

10. _____

What does this list of people have to tell me about the journaling group I would like to start?

_____

_____

_____

_____

_____

_____

_____

_____

_____

Here's a sketch of the invitation I'll send out to invite people to the first session:

Here's a letter I'll write to invite people to the first session:

What does this invitation and/or letter tell me about the journaling group I would like to start?

_____

_____

_____

_____

_____

The place for a journaling group is so important. This is a description of the ideal place:

_____

_____

_____

_____

_____

_____

_____

_____

_____

_____

_____

_____

_____

_____

_____

_____

_____

_____

What does the place I picked have to tell me about the journaling group I would like to start?

_____

_____

_____

The writing exercise I particularly like to start with is:

_____

_____

_____

Other journaling exercises I want to begin with are:

_____

_____

_____

_____

_____

_____

_____

The results I want are:

_____

_____

_____

_____

_____

_____

_____

_____

What do the above answers have to tell me about the type of journaling group I want to start?

_____

_____

_____

_____

_____

I am committed to my purpose of joining others to write because:

_____

_____

_____

_____

_____

When I read my journaling out loud I:

_____

_____

_____

_____

_____

_____

_____

_____

_____

_____

_____

_____

After a journal session with others I feel:

_____

_____

_____

What do the above answers have to tell me about my joining with others in a journaling group?

_____

_____

_____

_____

_____

THE LISTENER'S ROLE

A listener's role in a journaling group is a simple and special one: allowing, accepting, and being. Although it's a natural temptation to want to offer advice, a suggestion, or consolation, this kind of active listening can actually be harmful in a journaling group. The listener's participation should be limited to simply listening with interest. In this way the reader is given the integrity of owning and resolving their own work and the listener is given the chance to draw from that work as a wonderful way to generate further writing for their own benefit.

As a listener during a journaling group session this is what I noticed or observed in myself:

_____

_____

_____

_____

_____

_____